SADIQ
and the
Community
Garden

BY SIMAN NUURALI

ART BY CHRISTOS SKALTSAS

raintree

a Capstone company — publishers for children

Raintree is an imprint of Capstone Global Library Limited, a company incorporated in England and Wales having its registered office at 264 Banbury Road, Oxford, OX2 7DY – Registered company number: 6695582

www.raintree.co.uk
myorders@raintree.co.uk

Design by Tracy Davies
Design Element: Shutterstock/Irtsya
Original illustrations © Capstone Global Library Limited 2023
Originated by Capstone Global Library Ltd
Printed and bound in India

ISBN 978 1 3982 3955 5

British Library Cataloguing in Publication Data
A full catalogue record for this book is available from the British Library.

CONTENTS

FACTS ABOUT SOMALIA

- Somali people come from many different clans.
- Many Somalis are nomadic. That means they travel from place to place. They search for water, food and land for their animals.
- Somalia is mostly desert. It doesn't rain often there.
- The camel is an important animal to Somali people. Camels can survive a long time without food or water.
- Around ninety-nine per cent of all Somalis are Muslim.

SOMALI TERMS

baba (BAH-baah) a common word for father

habo (ha-boh) a female relative on your mother's side

hooyo (HOY-yoh) mother

qalbi (KUHL-bee) my heart

salaam (sa-LAHM) a short form of Arabic greeting, used by many Muslims. It also means "peace".

sambuus (sahm-BOOS) a fried pastry in the shape of a triangle that is filled with spicy meat or vegetables

wiilkeyga (wil-KAY-gaah) my son

CHAPTER 1

AN EMPTY PLOT

"Be careful, Rania," said *Baba*. "I don't want you to trip."

Baba, Sadiq and his little twin sisters were walking to the library. Rania and Amina were skipping ahead.

"Did you enjoy the book, Sadiq?" asked Baba. "It looks like a lot of fun!"

"I loved it, Baba," said Sadiq. "It's about a superhero. But his powers only work if someone calls his name."

"That sounds interesting," said Baba. "What will you take out today?"

"I will get the next one in the series," replied Sadiq. "There are eight in total. This is the second one."

"What's that?" asked Rania. She was squinting and pointing into the empty plot of land they were walking past.

"Where, *qalbi*?" asked Baba. "Do you see something?"

"I think so," said Rania. "But it's gone."

"It's a cat!" said Amina, running after it. "I see it too!"

"Be careful!" said Baba. He walked quickly to catch up with Amina. Just as he was getting close, Amina tripped over some old bricks.

"OW!" cried Amina. "OW! Baba, it hurts so much!"

"Let me see," said Baba, bending down. "Oh you scraped your knee, honey. We can get it cleaned up when we get home."

"Are you okay?" asked Sadiq. He helped Amina stand up.

"I think so," said Amina sadly. She had tears in her eyes.

"Here, take my hand," said Baba. "I don't want you to trip again."

"Why is this land empty, Baba?" asked Sadiq. "There's a lot of stuff lying around on the ground. I see litter and old boxes over there."

"I am not sure, *wiilkeyga*," said Baba. "It looks like it hasn't been used in a while. I don't think anyone's been looking after it."

Sadiq kept thinking about the empty land as they continued on to the library.

"Will you help me find a book, Sadiq?" asked Rania. She looked up at her brother and smiled.

"Of course I will," said Sadiq. "Would you like to come with us, Amina?"

"Yes! I want a book too," said Amina, excited. "My knee stopped hurting. Maybe there's a book about knees!"

"You're so funny, Amina," said Sadiq, laughing. He ruffled his sister's hair.

"Keep an eye on your sisters, Sadiq," Baba said. "Meet me here in about thirty minutes."

"Okay, Baba," Sadiq replied. "I know where my book is, so I'll be quick. I'll help the twins pick theirs out too."

Sadiq and his sisters walked towards the children's section.

"What do you want to read about?" Sadiq asked his sisters.

"Dinosaurs!" said Rania.

"Cute baby animals!" said Amina.

"Okay, let's see what we can find," said Sadiq.

Soon the kids were browsing and having fun picking books. There were so many to choose from!

"Come on, Rania and Amina," said Sadiq. "Baba will be waiting for us."

They walked towards the check-out desk.

"Did you find your books?" asked Baba.

"Yes," said Sadiq, smiling. "I found the third superhero book in the series! Rania wanted one about dinosaurs. And Amina got one about baby animals. We even found one about knees!"

Baba laughed. "I can't wait to read that one!" he said.

"What did you get, Baba?" asked Sadiq. "I really like the cover."

"Your *hooyo* wanted a gardening

book," said Baba. "We are getting ready for our spring planting."

"Can I help?" asked Sadiq excitedly. He loved helping his parents outside, especially when he could dig in the ground.

"Of course, wiilkeyga!" said Baba. "I am sure we could do with the help."

"Me too! Me too!" said Rania and Amina loudly.

"Okay, okay, you can help too," Baba whispered. "But we have to be quiet in the library."

Rania and Amina put their fingers to their lips and giggled.

CHAPTER 2

A TACO SALAD GARDEN

"Hooyo, can I have a plaster?" asked Amina. "My knee hurts again."

"What's wrong with your knee?" asked Hooyo as she fried *sambuus* on the hob.

"I tripped and fell," said Amina, pouting. "It hurt a lot. But I was very brave when Baba put medicine on it."

"Oh, I am sorry, qalbi," said Hooyo.

"Here, let me put a plaster on for you."

"She was running and tripped on some old bricks," explained Sadiq.

"We were walking to the library," added Baba. "There is an empty plot of land on the way. Amina saw a cat and ran after it."

"Oh, I know the land you mean," said Hooyo. "It would be a nice community space. I wish the council would fix it up."

"You are right," said Baba. "Something for everyone to enjoy."

"A playground!" said Rania excitedly.

"With swings!" said Amina, clapping.

"That would be fun," said Sadiq's older sister, Aliya. "But what about the grown-ups?"

"Swings are fun for everyone!" said Amina.

Aliya rolled her eyes, but she smiled.

"A skate park would be so great!" said Sadiq's brother, Nuurali. "I could learn to do an ollie on my skateboard."

"Those are good ideas," said Baba. "But they would cost the council a lot of money to build."

"How about a park?" said Sadiq. "With lots of trees and benches for people to sit. They could read books and enjoy nature."

"That would be so nice, qalbi," said Hooyo, smiling. "I can just imagine how relaxing it would be."

"Alright, everyone," said Baba as he brought the plates to the table. "We can talk about more ideas. But now it's time to eat veggie sambuus!"

***

The next day at school, Sadiq was in science class with his friends Zaza and Manny.

"I think the radishes look bigger," said Sadiq. "What do you guys think?"

"I think they look smaller," said Zaza, grinning.

"Very funny," said Manny. "You're right, Sadiq. I think they are bigger than last week."

"Ms Battersby says bigger leaves are a good sign," said Sadiq.

"Okay, class," said their teacher. "It's discussion time. Today's topic is: where do people get vegetables to eat?"

"From the supermarket," said Zayyan.

"Good answer, Zayyan," said Ms Battersby. "Where else?"

"From the farmer's market," said Spencer. "That's where my mum goes."

"Very good, Spencer," said Ms Battersby. "Anyone else?"

"Some people grow their own vegetables," said Manny.

"That's right, Manny!" said Ms Battersby. "Growing your own food can save money and build healthy eating habits! People can grow their own food if they have space."

"Like at a farm!" said Zaza. "But I have never been to one. And we don't have room for a garden at my house. My hooyo says our garden is too small."

"My hooyo and baba have a flower garden," said Sadiq. "They plant it in the spring. But just flowers, no vegetables."

"That sounds really nice, Sadiq," said Ms Battersby.

The bell rang, and Ms Battersby

dismissed the pupils for lunch.

The kids put away their books and headed to the canteen.

"Look, guys! Taco salad for lunch!" said Manny, pointing at the menu posted near the door.

"If I ever have a garden, I will grow a taco salad!" joked Zaza.

"You're so silly, Zaza!" said Sadiq, laughing.

CHAPTER 3

HOOYO HAS AN IDEA

"Is your mum picking us up?" asked Manny.

Sadiq, Manny and Spencer had stayed after school. They were making cards for kids in the hospital.

"Yes, she is," replied Sadiq. "She'll be here soon, so we should pack up."

"We can finish these tomorrow," said Spencer. He got up to put away the felt-tip pens.

"I will put these paper scraps in the recycling bin," said Sadiq. "You can put the cards on the side table, Manny."

"Thank you for cleaning up, boys," said Ms Battersby. "I will see you all tomorrow."

"Bye, Ms Battersby!" the boys called out together.

The boys walked out to the car park. Hooyo's car was already there.

"Hello, boys!" said Hooyo as they got into the car.

"*Salaam*, Hooyo!"

"Salaam, *habo*!"

"Hi, Mrs Dualle!"

"How was your day?" Hooyo asked as she pulled away.

"We're growing radishes and tomatoes for science class," said Sadiq. "We learned that some people grow their own food."

"Mmm, yum!" said Hooyo, smiling. "I love radishes! I hope I can get some when they are ready."

"Ms Battersby said some people have a garden," said Manny. "I wish I had a garden. I would grow my favourite food, sweet potatoes! But my mum says we don't have the space."

"How about you, Spencer?" asked Hooyo. She looked at him in the rear-view mirror. "What would you like to grow?"

"I would like to grow our own

tomatoes," said Spencer shyly. "It's for my mum's special Bolognese sauce. But I don't think my parents have time for a garden because they're so busy."

"That sounds like a wonderful idea, Spencer," said Hooyo. "I hope you can grow tomatoes one day."

"I wish we had room in our family garden," said Sadiq. "I would let you both grow your vegetables there."

"Thanks, Sadiq," said Spencer. "That's really cool of you!"

"Very cool," agreed Manny, grinning.

Soon they got to Manny and Spencer's street. They lived next door to each other.

"Thanks for the lift!" they called out.

"Do you think your friends would really like to grow a garden?" asked Hooyo after they had dropped off the boys.

"Yes!" replied Sadiq. "It's so much fun when we do it at school. They could grow their favourite foods."

"I might have an idea," said Hooyo, winking. "But you'll have to wait and see!"

"Oh, come on, Hooyo!" begged Sadiq. "Please tell me what it is."

Sadiq did not like waiting for surprises. But Hooyo wouldn't tell him her idea.

"You will have to be patient," she said, laughing.

"Finish your breakfast, Sadiq," said Baba. "Zaza's hooyo will be here soon to take you to school."

"I am almost ready, and my backpack is by the door," said Sadiq.

"Before you go . . . ," said Hooyo, coming into the kitchen. "Remember the idea I had?"

Sadiq eagerly looked up from his porridge. "Yes?"

"Well, I called the council about the empty plot of land," she said.

"The one we saw the other day?" asked Sadiq. He forgot all about his breakfast. He wondered what the land had to do with Hooyo's idea.

"Yes. Guess what I learned?" said Hooyo, smiling. "They said the land belongs to the council. And they're looking for volunteers to clean it up."

"I bet *we* could be volunteers!" said Sadiq. "I would love to help. So would Zaza and Manny and the other kids at school!"

"That's great, qalbi!" said Hooyo. "Will you ask them?"

"Yes, I will!" said Sadiq. "Was that the idea you had?"

"Part of it," replied Hooyo, smiling.

"Oh, please give me a clue, Hooyo!" said Sadiq.

"Okay, two more bites of porridge

first," she said.

Sadiq took two bites so big that his cheeks puffed out as he chewed.

"First clue: it's something everyone can use," said Hooyo. "Second clue: it's a way that everyone can grow their own vegetables."

"A garden . . . for everyone?" asked Sadiq. He leaped out of his chair. "Oh wait! *A community garden!*"

"Careful, wiilkeyga," said Baba, laughing. "You almost spilled your porridge."

"That's right, Sadiq," said Hooyo, laughing too. "We can start a community garden. Everyone in the area can have a section. They can grow

whatever they like."

"Really?" said Sadiq, jumping up and down. "Thank you, Hooyo! I can't wait to tell Manny and Spencer and Zaza!"

"But remember, Sadiq," said Hooyo. "There's clean-up work to be done first, and we'll need lots of help."

"Don't worry, Hooyo," said Sadiq. "I am on it. I will get volunteers!"

"Amina, can you please get me spinach out of the fridge?" asked Baba. "I am making smoothies to take to school."

"Spinach in smoothies, Baba?" asked Sadiq, surprised.

"Yes, why not?" replied Baba.

"Spinach is good for you. It will give you super strength! And you won't even notice it in your mango smoothie."

"I didn't know you could *drink* vegetables!" said Sadiq, shaking his head.

Baba laughed. He put the spinach in the blender and turned it on.

Just then, the doorbell rang. Sadiq ran to answer it.

"Oh hi, Zaza! You're early," said Sadiq.

"Only because I thought you'd be late," said Zaza, teasing.

"Ha ha, very funny," said Sadiq. He playfully punched Zaza's arm.

"Here's your smoothie, Sadiq," said Baba after he had put on the lid tightly. "It will stay cold till snack time."

Sadiq slid it in his backpack. "Thanks for the superhero smoothie, Baba!"

"Bye, Sadiq!" his family called after him.

CHAPTER 4

SADIQ RECRUITS HELPERS

Sadiq and Zaza got to school just in time. Sadiq could not wait to tell everyone about Hooyo's idea.

"Hello, third graders!" said Ms Battersby. "Let's check on the tomatoes today. They've been growing fast!"

Sadiq raised his hand.

"Yes, Sadiq," said Ms Battersby. "Did you have a question?"

"Not a question, Ms Battersby," said Sadiq, standing up. "I wanted to share my mum's idea with the class. It's about our science unit on growing vegetables!"

"Let's hear it, Sadiq," said Ms Battersby.

"There's an empty plot of land by the library," Sadiq explained. "It's got old and broken stuff lying around. My mum says we can make it into a community garden."

The class was quiet. Sadiq was worried they didn't like the idea.

"My mum called the council to ask," he continued. "If we can clean it up, we can have the garden. But we need volunteers to help."

"That's awesome, Sadiq!" Manny piped up. "I can finally grow sweet potatoes!"

"I can't wait to tell my mum," said Spencer. "She's going to love the tomatoes I'll grow for her Bolognese sauce!"

"Great idea, Sadiq," said Ms Battersby. "Why don't we plan it out on our whiteboard?"

The kids started chattering about all their ideas.

"We will need tools," said Ms. Battersby. "And adults to supervise. So your parents will have to be with you."

"My dad has lots of gardening tools," said Zayyan. "I can ask him to bring them."

"My mum offered to buy us vegetable seeds!" said Sadiq.

"I'll ask my dad to help too!" said Manny. "He's good at doing all kinds of stuff."

"I'll ask my parents to volunteer for the clean-up," said Spencer. "They love hearing my updates on our tomato and radish plants every day. I think they would like to grow some too!"

Soon, Ms Battersby's whiteboard was full of plans for the community garden.

***

Two weeks later, everyone gathered at the plot. It was a beautiful Saturday morning. Ms Battersby was wearing her gardening hat.

Sadiq, Zaza, Manny, Zayyan and Spencer were there with their parents. A couple of other pupils had also come with their parents.

Sadiq couldn't wait to get started. He was excited to see that so many volunteers had shown up!

"Okay, everyone, gather round," said Baba. "I want you all to be careful. There could be old nails and broken glass around. I don't want anyone to get hurt."

"Do you all have safety gloves?" asked Hooyo.

"Yes!" the group cheered loudly.

Then Hooyo and Baba explained the plan and gave the group instructions. They would pick up all the litter on the plot, being very careful with sharp things. Next, they would rake to pull up the weeds and prepare the soil for planting. Finally, they would mark out evenly sized sections for every family that wanted one.

Soon everyone got to work cleaning up the land.

"We can stack the bricks in the corner," said Baba, pointing. "Carry just two at a time, Sadiq. I don't want you to drop them on your foot."

"Okay, Baba," said Sadiq.

Sadiq knew he was strong enough to carry more. He had had a spinach mango smoothie for breakfast! But he followed Baba's instructions.

"Should I pull these out?" Spencer asked his dad, pointing at some fuzzy green plants. "I can't tell if they're weeds or not."

"Yes, those are weeds," his dad replied. "They're easy to pull. You can put them in this garden waste bag."

Ms. Battersby and Hooyo measured out each section. They made sure they left room for people to walk and get wheelchairs between sections.

Manny's dad put sticks at the corner of each section. Then he connected them with strings to make squares.

"Now we're ready to plant the seeds and water them!" Baba said.

The kids and their families got to

work, and soon all the seeds were in the ground. They had planted beans, squash, sweet potatoes, lettuce and lots more!

"I think that's all the seeds my hooyo brought," said Sadiq, looking around.

"What about all the extra sections?" asked Manny.

"Yeah, what should we do with them?" asked Zayyan.

Sadiq thought for a moment. "You know what's missing from our community garden? The community! Let's invite more people!" he said. "I think some of our neighbours would like to garden."

"I know my grandma would really like a section," said Manny. "Can I invite her to plant some vegetables?"

"That's a great idea, Manny," said Ms Battersby with a smile. "I think we have more work to do. Let's spread the word about our community garden!"

CHAPTER 5

THE COMMUNITY HELPERS!

It was a Monday afternoon, and Sadiq and his classmates were making posters in science class. The posters had information to let people around the community know about the new garden.

"Manny and Spencer, how is the sign coming along for the community garden entrance?" asked Sadiq.

"We're almost done, Sadiq," said Spencer. "We just need to colour it a bit more. And draw some plants and flowers on it."

The sign read in big letters:

The class had discussed what rules the garden should have. And Hooyo and Baba talked with the council about what rules they required:

Sign up for a section by contacting the council.

You can have your own garden section or share with your family or friends.

Please be careful when walking around the garden. Don't step inside other people's garden sections.

You can only work and plant in your section. You can help on another section if you have permission from the owner.

Pull any weeds by hand. This is a chemical-free garden!

Please keep the community garden clean. Don't litter – use the rubbish bin and garden waste bins.

Remember to have fun and look after our garden together!

The kids spent the rest of class finishing their posters and the sign.

"We should divide the posters among us," said Sadiq.

"Zaza, will you help me hang these after school?" asked Sadiq. "We can put ours up in the public library. I'll ask my mum to take us. I want to look for the next book in my superhero series, anyway!"

"Yeah! I will check out a book while I'm there too," said Zaza. "Maybe they have a superhero cookbook!"

"Spencer and I can go to the leisure centre," said Manny. "My dad is driving us home from school today, and he has to go there anyway."

"You've got it, partner!" said Spencer, grinning.

"Great teamwork, everyone!" said Ms. Battersby. "I will let the council know that we are ready to put up the sign at the community garden."

"Hey," said Spencer, who was checking on the class tomato plant. "Does anyone know how to fix a sliced tomato?"

Everyone shook their head.

"With tomato *paste*!" Spencer said with a grin.

***

A few weeks later, Sadiq went with Baba and his sisters to the new community garden.

"Look, Baba!" said Sadiq, pointing to their section. "I think my beans are sprouting!"

"You are right," said Baba, nodding. "The leaves are still very small, but they're coming up nicely."

"They're so tiny!" squealed Amina, pointing. "Cute baby plants!"

"Bean leaves aren't cute, Amina!" said Sadiq, laughing. But Amina insisted that they were.

"Isn't that Manny's grandmother?" asked Baba. "We should go and say salaam to her."

"I think so," said Sadiq, looking across the garden. "Manny was really excited she got a section. He told me at

COMMUNITY GARDEN
ALL ARE WELCOME HERE!

BEANS

school she was very happy. She's going to grow cucumbers!"

Baba, Sadiq and the girls walked over to say hello. They could see another family also planting near by.

"You and your friends should be very proud, wiilkeyga," said Baba. "This all started with an empty plot of land and a trip to the library for a superhero book. You all did such a great job!"

"Thank you, Baba," said Sadiq, puffing his chest. "You and Hooyo helped *A LOT!*"

Baba laughed at Sadiq's joke. "This is a much safer space now," he said. "And because of your hard work, the community has a garden. People can grow healthy food and save money!"

"You are a community superhero, Sadiq!" said Rania.

Sadiq laughed and high-fived his sister.

GLOSSARY

chemical-free not involving the use of a substance used in or produced by chemistry; medicines, gunpowder and some food stuff are all made from chemicals

dismiss allow or cause to leave

instruction outline of how something is to be done

measure find out the size or strength of something

ollie trick in which a skateboarder steps on the back of the board to make the board rise into the air

plaster covering that protects a wound

plot small area of planted ground

rearview mirror mirror in a vehicle that allows the driver to see what is behind the vehicle

recycling process of using things again instead of throwing them away

series group of related things or events that come one after another

sprout young plant that has just appeared above the soil

volunteer person who chooses to do work without pay

weed plant that grows where it is not wanted

TALK ABOUT IT

1. Sadiq and the volunteers planted many different vegetables, including beans, squash, sweet potatoes and lettuce. What would you plant if you had a community garden in your neighbourhood? Name five plants, vegetables or fruit that you would plant.

2. Imagine that the empty land hadn't become a community garden. Sadiq's family had many ideas on what the land could become. How would the story be different if it had become a playground, like Rania and Amina suggested, or another idea? What do you think the best use of the land would be?

3. Asking family members is one way that Sadiq and his classmates were able to gather volunteers to create the garden. Talk to a friend about some ideas you can think of to find volunteers for a community project.

WRITE IT DOWN

1. Sadiq and his friends helped contribute to their community in many ways, including helping with the community garden and writing letters to kids in the hospital. Write down three ways you can help your community.

2. Sadiq and his classmates made posters showing information about the new garden. Create a poster about a community project you would be interested in having in your area. Include details such as what the project is about and how it can help the community. Don't forget to decorate it!

3. Think about where you get your vegetables from. Draw the process you think your vegetables took to get to your plate. Include captions labelling the places your vegetables stopped along the way!

EAT THE RAINBOW!

What colour is your diet? Healthy foods are often brightly coloured, like the rainbow! For one week, keep track of the fruit, vegetables and other healthy foods you eat. Try to eat every colour of the rainbow! On a chart, keep track of the colours of the healthy foods you eat each day. (P.S. Sweets don't count!)

WHAT YOU NEED:

- sheet of paper
- felt-tip pens or crayons
- ruler

WHAT TO DO:

1. Turn the paper lengthwise. Draw a box that is 20 cm (8 in) across and 18 cm (7 in) down.

2. Inside the box, draw a grid of 2.5 x 2.5-cm (1 x 1-in) squares. You will have 56 squares.

3. Leave the first square blank. Then across the top row, write the name of each day of the week in the boxes, starting with Monday.

starting with Monday.

4. In the first column on the left, leave the first square blank again, then fill in each box below with the name of a rainbow colour: red, orange, yellow, green, blue, purple.

5. For each day of the week, keep track of what you eat. Try to eat fruit and vegetables with rainbow colours! Write down the food items you eat each day in the colour row they belong in. (For example, a plum would go in the purple row.)

6. Invite your family to join you in eating the rainbow! Ask to go along to the supermarket and see what colourful healthy foods you can find. Add some fresh colour to your plate!

	MONDAY	TUESDAY	WEDNESDAY	THURSDAY	FRIDAY	SATURDAY	SUNDAY
RED		apple					
ORANGE	orange juice						
YELLOW	yellow pepper	banana smoothie					
GREEN	lettuce	cucumber					
BLUE	blueberry yogurt						
PURPLE		grapes					

CREATORS

Siman Nuurali grew up in Kenya. She now lives in Minnesota, USA. Siman and her family are Somali – just like Sadiq and his family! She and her five children love to play badminton and board games together. Siman works at Children's Hospital of Minnesota and, in her free time, she enjoys writing and reading.

Christos Skaltsas was born and raised in Athens, Greece. For the past fifteen years, he has worked as a freelance illustrator for children's book publishers. In his free time, he loves playing with his son, collecting vinyl records and travelling around the world.